YORK NOTES

Talking in Whispers

James Watson

Notes by Brian Conroy

Longman   York Press

YORK PRESS
322 Old Brompton Road, London SW5 9JH

ADDISON WESLEY LONGMAN LIMITED
Edinburgh Gate, Harlow,
Essex CM20 2JE, United Kingdom
Associated companies, branches and representatives throughout the world

First published 1997

ISBN 0–582–31527–1

Illustrated by Chris Price,
Designed by Vicki Pacey, Trojan Horse
Typeset by Pantek Arts, Maidstone, Kent
Phototypeset by Gem Graphics, Trenance, Mawgan Porth, Cornwall
Produced by Longman Asia Limited, Hong Kong

C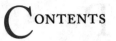ONTENTS

Preface		4
PART ONE		
INTRODUCTION	How to Study a Novel	5
	James Watson's Background	6
	Context & Setting	9
PART TWO		
SUMMARIES	General Summary	14
	Detailed Summaries, Comment,	
	Glossaries & Tests	16
	Chapters 1–2	16
	Chapter 3	20
	Chapters 4–5	23
	Chapters 6–7	27
	Chapter 8 and Epilogue	31
PART THREE		
COMMENTARY	Themes	34
	Structure	40
	Characters	40
	Language & Style	45
PART FOUR		
STUDY SKILLS	How to Use Quotations	47
	Essay Writing	48
	Sample Essay Plan & Questions	51
PART FIVE		
CULTURAL CONNECTIONS		
	Broader Perspectives	53
Literary Terms		54
Test Answers		55

PREFACE

York Notes are designed to give you a broader perspective on works of literature studied at GCSE and equivalent levels. We have carried out extensive research into the needs of the modern literature student prior to publishing this new edition. Our research showed that no existing series fully met students' requirements. Rather than present a single authoritative approach, we have provided alternative viewpoints, empowering students to reach their own interpretations of the text. York Notes provide a close examination of the work and include biographical and historical background, summaries, glossaries, analyses of characters, themes, structure and language, cultural connections and literary terms.

If you look at the Contents page you will see the structure for the series. However, there's no need to read from the beginning to the end as you would with a novel, play, poem or short story. Use the Notes in the way that suits you. Our aim is to help you with your understanding of the work, not to dictate how you should learn.

York Notes are written by English teachers and examiners, with an expert knowledge of the subject. They show you how to succeed in coursework and examination assignments, guiding you through the text and offering practical advice. Questions and comments will extend, test and reinforce your knowledge. Attractive colour design and illustrations improve clarity and understanding, making these Notes easy to use and handy for quick reference.

York Notes are ideal for:
• Essay writing
• Exam preparation
• Class discussion

The author of these Notes is Brian Conroy (BA Hons) who teaches English at Ryton Comprehensive School in the Tyne Valley. Brian has been involved with GCSE as a senior examiner since the outset and is currently a Principal Examiner for NEAB. From 1998 he will be a Principal Examiner on the new post-16 syllabus for NEAB.

The text used in these Notes is the Collins Tracks edition, 1986.

Health Warning: **This study guide will enhance your understanding, but should not replace the reading of the original text and/or study in class.**

PART ONE

INTRODUCTION

HOW TO STUDY A NOVEL

You have bought this book because you wanted to study a novel on your own. This may supplement classwork.

- You will need to read the novel several times. Start by reading it quickly for pleasure, then read it slowly and carefully. Further readings will generate new ideas and help you to memorise the details of the story.
- Make careful notes on themes, plot and characters of the novel. The plot will change some of the characters. Who changes?
- The novel may not present events chronologically. Does the novel you are reading begin at the beginning of the story or does it contain flashbacks and a muddled time sequence? Can you think why?
- How is the story told? Is it narrated by one of the characters or by an all-seeing ('omniscient') narrator?
- Does the same person tell the story all the way through? Or do we see the events through the minds and feelings of a number of different people.
- Which characters does the narrator like? Which characters do you like or dislike? Do your sympathies change during the course of the book? Why? When?
- Any piece of writing (including your notes and essays) is the result of thousands of choices. No book had to be written in just one way: the author could have chosen other words, other phrases, other characters, other events. How could the author of your novel have written the story differently? If events were recounted by a minor character how would this change the novel?

Studying on your own requires self-discipline and a carefully thought-out work plan in order to be effective. Good luck.

Education and work record

James Watson was born on 8 November 1936 in Darwen, Lancashire. He was educated at the University of Nottingham, graduating with a BA degree in history in 1958. Between 1958–60 he served as lieutenant in the Royal Army Education Corps.

He had a fairly varied career after leaving the army, though we may notice that all his jobs were concerned, directly or indirectly, with literature and education. From 1960–1 he taught English in Milan, Italy, as one of the staff of the British Council there. From 1961–3 he worked as a journalist and more particularly as an art critic on the *Northeast Evening Gazette* in Middlesbrough, Yorkshire.

From 1963–5 he was education officer with the Dunlop Company in London, and since 1966 he has been Lecturer in Communication at West Kent College, Tonbridge, as well as course director of a Media and Communications study programme, working in collaboration with the University of Greenwich. His twin interests, literature and education, are reflected in his professional career, and also in his return to academic study in 1977–8, when he took an MA in Education at the University of Sussex, Brighton.

Early steps in writing

His career as a writer began in 1967 with the publication of a historical novel for young people, *Sign of the Swallow* (Nelson), set in the Renaissance period and thus reflecting the author's historical training. His second novel, *The Bull Leapers* (Gollancz, 1970), is a reworking of the Greek Theseus myth and of the Cretan legend of the Minotaur. Watson's third novel, *Legion of the White Tiger* (Gollancz, 1973), is again set in the distant past, describing the clash of two cultures, the invading Huns against the disintegrating Roman Empire.

After these three novels Watson's interest turned to more recent events in Europe and beyond. His aim is no longer only to entertain and possibly to instruct; he wants to awaken his readers' concern for the world around them. His young heroes and heroines are there for his readers to identify with and so indirectly to become aware of each young individual's potential for influencing the course of events which they are witnessing. This may be the key to his popularity with his readership: his ability to encourage the emotional and intellectual involvement of young people in the present-day world.

James Watson's main body of work consists of novels set around the experiences of young people today.

The first of these novels, *The Freedom Tree* (Gollancz, 1976), is set mostly in Spain during the Civil War of 1936–9, but touches also on the Depression in Britain. The young hero, Will, comes from Jarrow (famous for the 1933 march of the unemployed to London). His father died fighting for the Republican side in the Spanish Civil War, and Will too makes his way to Spain with a group of friends. Only two of them, Will and Molly, a nurse, survive the journey, arriving in Guernica in time to witness the destruction of the little town by German bombers sent to aid the Spanish fascists.

Talking in Whispers came next. It is set in Chile during the dictatorship of the generals. The young hero, Andres, is much more directly involved in the political events he witnesses than Will had been. Andres possesses photographic evidence that the Secret Service had carried out the murder of an opponent of the junta, and he finds the courage to make the evidence public in the face of threats and torture. The author's dedication of the novel to Amnesty International underlines his own commitment to the cause of political freedom.

Watson's next novel, *Where Nobody Sees* (Gollancz, 1987), finds the forces of the dark at work in Britain as well.

The young protagonists are Luke, a badger-watcher, and Petra, a member of a community theatre group (the introduction of a girl heroine is as significant and timely as Luke's passionate protective interest in nature). They discover that nuclear waste is being dumped in the woods near Luke's home, and eventually, employing the dramatically effective method of a theatrical performance, they succeed in making their discovery public, not without considerable risk to themselves from the mercenaries involved in the dumping.

More recent work After a collection of short stories, *Make Your Move* (Gollancz, 1988), came another novel, *No Surrender* (Collins Lions, 1992), set in Angola at the time of the free elections in Namibia. The main characters are Hamish, a white South African, and Malenga, the daughter of a local black politician. Their capture by guerillas gives the novel its tension and sense of danger. The book is dedicated to the people of Angola.

In his most recent novel, *Ticket to Prague* (Gollancz, 1993), Watson returns to Europe. The story combines cleverly and successfully two discrete themes of violence: the racial tensions in Britain and the menacing undercurrents in the Czech Republic after the Velvet Revolution when the agents of the old Communist regime strove to cover up their past, using any means to hand.

After her involvement in a fight with British skinheads Amy, the heroine, is sentenced to community service in a mental institution. There she meets Josef, a Czech exile who has not spoken for twenty years. Amy manages to break Josef's silence and discovers that he is a famous dissident poet. They go to Prague together, accompanied by a British television crew eager for a scoop. Amy succeeds in carrying out Josef's wish, to tell the truth about those who had betrayed him and others.

The novel is a close parallel of events in the life of the Czech poet Ivan Blatny and his English friend Frances Meacham, a fact acknowledged by Watson in the dedication to the novel.

Watson has also written several radio plays: *Gilbert Makepeace Lives!* (1972); *Venus Rising from the Sea* (1977); *A Slight Insurrection* (1980); *What a Little Moonlight Can Do* (1982); and a radio adaptation (1993) of his novel *No Surrender*.

The common theme in James Watson's work is the individual's striving for better understanding, clearer vision, and ultimately a better world. As we will see James Watson imply in *Talking in Whispers*, education and books do matter because in Watson's own words 'No frontiers can keep out the song of the poet' *(Ticket to Prague)*.

CONTEXT & SETTING

James Watson's story is set in the South American country of Chile. The book was written in 1983 and the writer says that it is set 'somewhere between the present and the future'. As such we can accept that it is in our own time; there are many contemporary governments and societies which match those described by James Watson.

HISTORICAL CONTEXT

The history of Chile is representative of many of its neighbouring countries in South and Central America. It is a long stretch of land on the Pacific coast of South America, bounded by Peru and Bolivia to the north and the huge landmass of Argentina to the east. Its native population is Indian, almost a million in number, principally the Araucanian Indians. This tribe took the lead in resisting the invading Spanish in the sixteenth and seventeenth centuries but their resistance was

crushed and the Spanish added the dominance of Chile
to that of other South American countries. It is a
chance encounter with an Araucanian Indian, and a
respect for their pride and dignity, which helps to
stiffen Andres's resolve in Chapter 2.

Chile finally won its independence from Spain in 1817
under the leadership of Bernardo O'Higgins. British
business replaced Spanish domination with its eyes on
the nitrate and copper mines. However, British influences
declined under American competition and by the 1950s
American firms dominated Chile's main industries.

Social context

The dominance by leading American companies
produced divided ideas among the Chileans. The
companies themselves were vast multinational
organisations. They invested levels of finance and
technical expertise way above anything that could have
been invested by the Chilean government. Certainly the
investment of these companies relieved unemployment
and brought additional revenue to the government
through taxes and profits. However, there was always a
feeling among the Chilean workers that the vast global
firms gained massively from their investment. Their
gains were helped by the payment of low wages and the
subsequent low costing of materials exported back to
the United States. There are references in the book to
poverty and the huge gap between rich and poor.

As ever in these situations, where a native population
feels repressed and cheated by an outsider, the backlash
finally came. The first signs came with a wave of strikes
in the late 1960s mainly protesting at poor wages and
working conditions. Elections were due in 1970 and the
groups who led the strikes formed a party called

Popular Unity. Its leader was Salvador Allende. The main points of its campaign were nationalisation of key industries, free health care and education for all, better housing and the redistribution of land. These ideas, based on restoring Chile to its own people, helped Popular Unity to be the largest single party in the 1970 election, winning 37% of the vote. It is reasonable to assume that, in the novel, the Silver Lion, Miguel Alberti, believed in similar ideas and that the election rallies of Allende were similar to that described in the opening of the novel.

Since they had no overall majority, and could be outvoted by other parties acting together, Popular Unity found it difficult to push through all the reforms it had promised. However, success was achieved with production, employment, inflation and social benefits such as health care. Most notably, all the copper mines and banks became nationalised and were owned by the Chilean people. The owners received full value compensation but had to pay back a percentage of all the profits they had taken from Chile over the years. These actions set alarm bells ringing in the big North American firms, not only at the economic loss but at the possible expansion of Chile's policies into other South American countries where there was a significant US business presence. In Chapter 7 Jack Normanton makes direct comparisons between the situation in Chile and that in other South American countries such as El Salvador, Guatemala, Nicaragua and Bolivia.

CIA involvement and the military coup
The American response was subtle and, at first, secret. It used its own secret service, the Central Intelligence Agency (CIA), in a process called Destabilisation. The object was to undermine confidence in Popular Unity. The CIA used economic policies, propaganda, infiltration of trades unions and military support to the opposition to help destabilise the Allende government.

Despite the CIA programme funding anti-government propaganda and crippling strikes, Allende won a second election in 1973. At this point army leaders opposed to Allende, backed by the US, determined to bring down Popular Unity by force. On 29 June 1973 some army groups surrounded the presidential palace and called for the entire armed forces to join them. In spite of some help from loyal troops, the government finally fell in September after tanks moved into the capital, Santiago, and aircraft bombed the presidential palace. President Allende remained in the palace and died in the attack. Like the Silver Lion, Miguel Alberti, he paid with his life for opposing the military backed by US commercial interests and the CIA.

Life after the coup

The military rule which followed met widespread resistance. However, the army repression was brutal; over 10,000 Chileans died and over 150,000 were jailed and tortured in the months that followed. In Chapter 2 we are told what happened to Juan after the death of Allende; imprisonment for a year without charge. People who supported Popular Unity were victimised and trades unions banned. In the novel we see the same things happening to the followers of Miguel after his assassination. Most disturbing of all were the number of people arrested and never heard of again. This was the fate of Juan and the people Andres sees being executed by the soldiers at the end of Chapter 4 – they were called the 'Disappeared'. About half a million Chileans fled the country, some settling in Britain.

The economic reforms which followed, guided by the US, were disastrous for the majority of Chileans. Unemployment rose, education and health care became expensive and prices rose. Censorship of liberal views dominated the media. Recent years have seen some reforms but resistance continues even though trade and financial support, from the US and Western Europe, have enabled the military junta government, as depicted in the novel, to remain in force.

The continuing power of the junta is helped by several factors. Fear is a principal factor – well illustrated in the novel – since people still die or disappear like Juan, Father Mariano and Horacio. Protest marches are often attacked by the army or the police. Self-help groups and consistent support are helping to overcome the fear. Poverty is a second factor. Again, organisation of common funds is helping out. People are beginning to reform into trades unions. The role of women is paramount in the resurgence of opposition. As Isa does in the novel with her free school, they run many of the self-support systems and embarrass the army with demonstrations. Armed resistance, as exemplified in the novel by Hernando Salas, does exist; although their methods have differing levels of support, their personal courage is beyond reproach. As readers of *Talking In Whispers* these advances should not surprise us. We are constantly reminded that the finer things of human life – love, friendship, music and courage – survive even in a regime so oppressive as that depicted in the novel.

PART TWO

SUMMARIES

GENERAL SUMMARY

The book is set in the country of Chile and covers a period of seven days concentrating particularly on the lives of three young people, Andres and the twins, Isa and Beto. It deals with their attempts to publish photographic evidence of the violence of the government troops and the killing of the leader of the opposition, Miguel Alberti, the Silver Lion.

Chapters 1–2:
Death ... the
fightback
begins

Andres escapes from an ambush after his father is arrested and their companion is killed. He is picked up by Isa and Beto who are on their way to the election rally of the Silver Lion. On arriving at their destination they discover that the Silver Lion has been shot and the Communists blamed. On their return to the capital, Santiago, Andres finds that friends of his family have disappeared. He sees one friend, Braulio, being ill-treated by the police. As he gets closer he sees an American photographer, Don Chailey, filming the incidents. Don is arrested and Andres escapes with his camera and film.

Chapter 3:
A plan is
formed

Andres and his friends take the film to an acquaintance, Diego, who owns a printing press. The developed photographs show not only the violence of the soldiers but also evidence that Miguel was assassinated by a government agent. The friends agree to publish the pictures and set up a plan to recover some of Diego's printing equipment.

Chapters 4–5:
The plan
works ... but
then capture

Andres and the twins put the plan into action and, after some problems, escape from the station with the equipment. However, they are followed by the security services. Andres leaves the others and hides the printing equipment. While making his way to safety Andres

y

witnesses the execution of two lorry loads of prisoners by some soldiers. Among them is Don Chailey and Andres recovers his US press card. He reaches a seminary where he has been told he will be safe. He is taken in by Father Mariano and Sister Teresa. In the middle of the night a wounded resistance fighter is brought in. The security arrive, Andres tries to escape but is captured.

Chapters 6–7: Horror and evil in the House of Laughter

Andres is taken to the dreaded House of Laughter and cruelly tortured. He manages to hold out and is saved further punishment by the death of Father Mariano who gave nothing away. He is dumped outside the city and rescued by a farmer, Francisco, and his daughter, Rosa. Meanwhile one of Don's fellow journalists, Jack Normanton, has arrived in Chile and started to ask questions. He meets Isa and acquires copies of Don's films.

Chapter 8 and Epilogue.: Final triumph

Francisco and Rosa take Andres to a market where he knows Isa and Beto will be giving one of their puppet shows. He is hidden in their van and is finally reunited with them on the spot where they first met. The novel ends at a football match between England and Chile. Jack Normanton's paper has published the pictures and the copies printed by Diego are handed to the crowd. The truth is finally out.

DETAILED SUMMARIES

CHAPTER 1   The novel opens with an account of a political pre-election rally. It is addressed by Miguel Alberti, the Silver Lion, leader of the opposition to the military junta government. A twin brother and sister, Beto and Isa, are in the crowd which is optimistic about the result of the election, due the next day.

How does the writer create an atmosphere of fear and violence in this chapter?

The scene changes to an ambush on a car carrying members of a musical group. One member, Horacio, is dead but a father, Juan, has been captured, while his son, Andres, is desperately trying to escape. His father is taken away and we find that they are supporters of Miguel. We also discover that Andres's mother, Helen, was British and that the other member of the group, Braulio, is waiting for them in the town of San José.

Andres is picked up by Beto and Isa in the van they use to give puppet shows. They try to make their way to San José for Miguel's final speech before the election. Outside of town they hear that Miguel has been shot dead and the Communists blamed. They head back to Santiago, but in the suburbs, they run into a street gun battle. The chapter ends with the rumble of tanks on the streets of Santiago. The elections have been postponed indefinitely.

COMMENT   Despite the fast moving, action-packed storyline, and the pervading atmosphere of fear and panic, the writer still finds time to dwell on youthful interests – music, street theatre and boy–girl attraction. Notice how the physical descriptions concentrate on the beauty and athleticism of the young people.

We see the vicious attitudes of the security police and their diversion of blame over the shooting of Miguel. Notice how the radio broadcast swiftly clamps down on civil liberties, an echo of the reactions of the military junta after the 1973 coup (see Context and Setting).

y

GLOSSARY   **dove** the dove is often a symbol of peace
                charango a South American folk instrument, similar to a
                guitar
                Allende president of Chile at the time of the army coup in
                1973. He died in the attack on the presidential palace (see
                Context and Setting)

CHAPTER 2   In contrast to Chapter 1, where the opening is an optimistic rally in the stadium, Chapter 2 opens with a picture of the National Stadium being used as a detention centre for political prisoners.

Andres awakes in the remains of a mill occupied by Beto and Isa. We are given background information on his early family life and the death of his mother, Helen, in mysterious circumstances. Beto shows Andres the

Notice how the government uses the media for propaganda.

paper reporting the death of himself (Andres) and his father, Juan Larreta. Andres resolves to tell Juan's friends that Juan was taken prisoner and not killed. He also intends to track down Braulio and to let Horacio's parents and family know of his death. As he heads for their homes, he witnesses the shooting of a young man by the Black Berets.

However, none of the family and friends can be found; they have all disappeared, another echo of events after the 1973 coup (see Context and Setting). Finally,

Andres sees Braulio being taken into the National Stadium. As he tries to reach him, he latches on to an American pressman, Don Chailey, taking pictures of the brutality. Don is seen by the security men and beaten to the ground. Andres escapes with his camera and film.

COMMENT In this chapter we see Andres acquiring determination and a sense of purpose. Although frightened and unsure at the start, he is strengthened by the memories of his family and he resolves to let Juan's friends know that he was not killed as reported. He is further encouraged by the encounter with the Araucano Indian and by his association with the American.

The growing young love of Andres and Isa is a beacon of hope among the fear and violence.

We are given some indication of the power of literature in inspiring resistance. A poem by Chico Buarque is in Andres's mind as his resolve stiffens. A quotation from the work of Pablo Neruda, Chile's best loved poet, changes his mood to a more optimistic one.

GLOSSARY **Amnesty International** a non-political organisation dedicated to bringing attention to the abuse of human rights around the world, particularly the torture and jailing of political prisoners

House of Laughter the chillingly ironic title given to the detention cells of the secret police

Avenida Bernardo O'Higgins one of the main streets of Santiago, named after the hero of Chile's struggle for independence from the Spanish

Black Berets military enforcers who act alongside the Chilean police. The name reminds us of the Black Shirts, the British right wing movement of the 1930s. They are instantly associated with casual violence

Y

A — Identify the speaker.

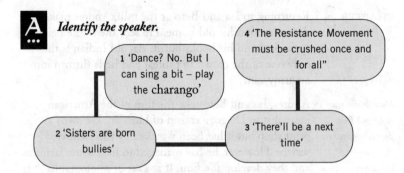

1 'Dance? No. But I can sing a bit – play the charango'

4 'The Resistance Movement must be crushed once and for all"

2 'Sisters are born bullies'

3 'There'll be a next time'

Identify the person 'to whom' this comment refers.

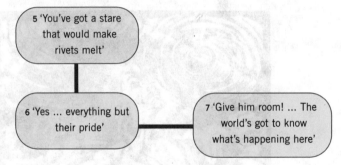

5 'You've got a stare that would make rivets melt'

6 'Yes ... everything but their pride'

7 'Give him room! ... The world's got to know what's happening here'

Check your answers on page 55.

B — Consider these issues.

a The contrasting moods established by the writer in the early part of Chapter 1.

b The early relationship built up between Andres, Isa and Beto.

c The reaction of the government to the death of Miguel Alberti.

d Andres's memories of his family; the significance of his mother.

e The growing determination of Andres and his awareness of his position as he searches for Braulio and his father's friends.

f The purpose of the references to poetry and song to underline the importance of the arts in a free society.

A PLAN IS FORMED

CHAPTER 3   Returning to Isa and Beto at the mill, Andres makes a
detour around his old home. He sees the house being
ransacked and his books burnt. An old Indian is the
only one of the crowd to protest and he is thrown into
an army van.

How do you react   Andres, Isa and Beto take the film of the American
to Diego? How   journalist to Diego, a cousin of Horacio. He owns a
does he contrast to   print shop but it has been wrecked by the security
the younger   service. However, he has managed to hide some facilities
characters?   and they develop the film. It is a set of photographs
which indicate that Miguel was assassinated by a
member of the security service, not the Communists.

They agree to publish the pictures. Diego formulates a
plan to recover and reassemble one of his printing
presses.

COMMENT   In this chapter the author clearly associates the
government of the military junta in Chile with one of
the most notorious repressive governments of all, that
of Nazi Germany. The burning of Juan's books and the
blaming of the murder of Miguel on the Communists,
thus giving the junta an excuse for the repression of
liberal views, reflect two of the most memorable

symbols of Nazi Germany; the regular book burnings and the fire at the German parliament, the Reichstag, which was started by the Nazis but blamed on the Communists.

Notice the type of books owned by Juan and what they tell us of his character. They all reflect civilised values, opposition to repression, Western European influences and revolutionary heroes. Even the presence of *Alice in Wonderland* is significant; it is a fantasy, an escape from harsh reality. Also, importantly for Andres, it had been a present from his mother.

GLOSSARY **William Blake** an English poet noted for his radicalism and his opposition to repressive government

Simon Bolivar South American revolutionary figure. Bolivia is named after him

A Identify the speaker.

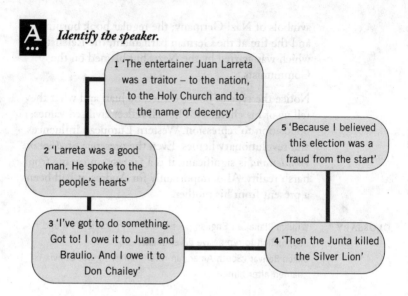

1 'The entertainer Juan Larreta was a traitor – to the nation, to the Holy Church and to the name of decency'

2 'Larreta was a good man. He spoke to the people's hearts'

3 'I've got to do something. Got to! I owe it to Juan and Braulio. And I owe it to Don Chailey'

4 'Then the Junta killed the Silver Lion'

5 'Because I believed this election was a fraud from the start'

Identify the person 'to whom' this comment refers.

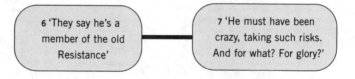

6 'They say he's a member of the old Resistance'

7 'He must have been crazy, taking such risks. And for what? For glory?'

Check your answers on page 55.

B Consider these issues.

a The way Juan was regarded by his neighbours.

b The way in which the author presents the character of Diego as a counter-balance to the younger characters.

c The significance of Don Chailey's photographs.

CHAPTER 4   Again the chapter opens with a reference to the prisoners in the National Stadium.

Identify the language features which maintain pace and tension in the scene at the station.

The action then switches to the carrying out of Diego's plan to recover the parts of his printing press. He has arranged for his contacts to deliver them to left-luggage lockers in the main station. On the way out they will drop the keys, with some money, into a collection held by Isa as her puppets perform. Andres, dressed as a porter, would retrieve the keys and unlock the left-luggage lockers. He would wheel the contents out of the station and quickly load them into a van driven by Beto.

Despite a few frights they manage to execute the plan but then find themselves followed by a truck belonging to the security forces. They hatch an escape plan and Andres manages to escape from Beto's van with the parts of the printing press. Isa and Beto continue into the town of Puente Alto and prepare to give a puppet performance for the school children.

Although injured, Andres prepares to hide the printing press when he hears the sound of army trucks. He witnesses the execution of two truck loads of prisoners.

THE PLAN WORKS ... BUT THEN CAPTURE

COMMENT   The implementation of Diego's plan and the
subsequent escape from Santiago is exciting. We can
imagine the tension and fear of the young people but it
is still, to them, an adventure. However, this escapade is
in stark contrast to the real evil of the mass murder
which Andres witnesses at the end of the chapter.
Escaping down mountain roads in a van is one thing,
witnessing the real evils of a repressive government
quite another.

Although Juan has disappeared at the start of the novel
we are constantly reminded of him, as if the author
wants us to remember, to stop him becoming one of the
'Disappeared' like so many of his fellow countrymen
(see Context and Setting). In this chapter Beto's song,
as they drive away from the station, and Andres's
thoughts, just before he hears the trucks at the end of
the chapter, bring Juan, and his possible situation, back
into our minds.

CHAPTER 5   Andres searches through the dead prisoners, afraid that
one may be Juan. He does not find Juan but he does
find the body of Don Chailey with his press card intact.
He collects identification from the other bodies and
then heads for the Seminary of Our Lady Of Mercy
where Isa and Beto have told him he can be helped by
Father Mariano.

Meanwhile Beto and Isa have finished their
performance for the schoolchildren. They find out, from
a newspaper, that there has been a major battle with
resistance fighters in Santiago and that the city is now
on full alert for opponents of the military junta.

Andres initially
mistrusts Father
Mariano.

At the seminary Andres puts his trust in Father
Mariano and shows him the identification from the
dead bodies. He sees a wounded resistance fighter
arrive, Father Mariano leave in disguise and return with
a female doctor to treat the wounded man.

In the early hours the seminary is raided by Black Berets. It appears that the wounded man is Hernando Salas, a leading resistance fighter. Father Mariano is beaten up and Andres tries to escape. However, he is found by the Black Berets.

COMMENT   This chapter indicates the role of the church in a repressive government. The comments on the Archbishop reveal that the junta has the support of church leaders for their style of government. However, at the lower levels of the church, there is active humanitarian support for the resistance fighters. Isa's comment on hanging a flag from the window also emphasises the support of the well-off for the regime. We see that the repressive government is an alliance of army, wealthy people and the church.

By his own admission, Andres grows from a boy to a man at the start of this chapter. Unlike many of his contemporaries in the macho societies of South America, this occurs through the experience of death rather than human love.

GLOSSARY   **worker priests** there is a tradition, in South American countries, of priests working in factories and industries alongside their parishioners
Valparaiso one of the major sea ports of Chile

TEST YOURSELF (Chapters 4–5)

 A *Identify the speaker.*

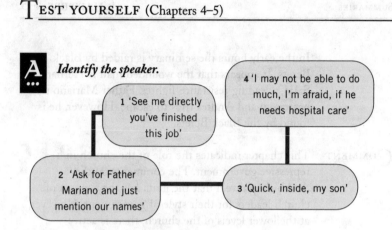

1 'See me directly you've finished this job'

4 'I may not be able to do much, I'm afraid, if he needs hospital care'

2 'Ask for Father Mariano and just mention our names'

3 'Quick, inside, my son'

Identify the person 'to whom' this comment refers.

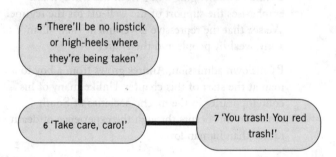

5 'There'll be no lipstick or high-heels where they're being taken'

6 'Take care, caro!'

7 'You trash! You red trash!'

Check your answers on page 55.

B *Consider these issues.*

a The use of the National Stadium at the start of Chapter 4 in contrast to the opening scene of the novel.

b The dramatic use of the incidents with the young girls and the old lady at the station.

c The contrast between the excitement of the escape and what Andres sees at the end of Chapter 4.

d The significance of the continuing references to Juan and his songs.

e Andres saying goodbye to childhood.

f Why the soldiers were so careless as to leave identification on the dead.

g The help which is available to those who do resist.

y

CHAPTER 6

How do you react to the details of Andres's treatment in the House of Laughter?

Mass arrests continue in Chile after the gun battle. Isa has a premonition that Andres has been captured. She confesses to Beto that she has a second set of Don Chailey's photographs hidden in their van.

Andres is split off with a small group of prisoners and taken to the House of Laughter. He is beaten as he tries to cover his movements and hide his identity. The interrogators seem to think that he has a message from Father Mariano and are interested in Salas, the wounded resistance fighter.

Isa visits the seminary and Sister Teresa gives her the identification of the dead men that Andres had left behind. Back at the House of Laughter Andres faces torture by electric shock.

COMMENT

In this chapter we have a graphic description of the capture and interrogation. It is worth noting the steps of degradation and the isolation. The two security policemen have appropriate names, one violent physically and the other clever with his questions. We see how difficult it is for Andres to keep talking whilst trying to maintain lies. The final descent to torture, after the beatings, is inevitable.

The opening paragraph gives us a view of how evil can spread in society, the vigilantes following up and looting after the Death Squads.

Isa's confession of love for Andres stands as a beacon of hope in a chapter of violence and misery. It is a reminder that finer feelings can survive among the fear and inhumanity.

CHAPTER 7

Jack Normanton, a fellow journalist, has arrived in Chile to seek information on Don Chailey. Isa gets in touch and arranges a meeting.

Andres manages to survive the electric shock torture.
He is saved by the death in custody of Father Mariano.
He has died without talking and has not revealed
Andres's identity. Isa meets Jack Normanton and hands
over Don Chailey's belongings and photographs. Jack
tells her to keep the camera for Andres.

How does the
behaviour of
Francisco and Rosa
alter the tone of the
chapter?

Andres is bundled into a lorry and driven out of the
city. He is dumped with a bundle of corpses in an area
called San Miguel. He is helped by a farmer, Francisco,
and his eight-year-old daughter, Rosa. Francisco's son,
Tonio, had been killed by the 'Security'. Although
injured, Andres is determined to get to the commune of
San Miguel as he knows Isa and Beto are due to give a
puppet show there.

COMMENT The character of the Snake, as we see him during the
torture of Andres is that of an inhuman madman. He
wants total control of all people and sees enemies
everywhere. He is presented as typical of the servants
of repressive regimes – cold, inhuman and totally mad.
These characters are a reflection of the government
they serve.

The early part of the chapter has an almost dramatic quality as it switches from scenes of torture to the outside world. The author wants to increase our awareness of the terrible contrast between the plight of Andres and the everyday life of the city.

GLOSSARY   **Santiaguena** a female inhabitant of Santiago
El Salvador a Central American country with a history of US involvement similar to Chile
El Plomo a mountain in the Andes

TEST YOURSELF (Chapters 6–7)

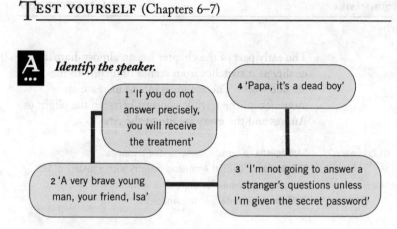

A Identify the speaker.

1 'If you do not answer precisely, you will receive the treatment'

4 'Papa, it's a dead boy'

2 'A very brave young man, your friend, Isa'

3 'I'm not going to answer a stranger's questions unless I'm given the secret password'

Identify the person 'to whom' this comment refers.

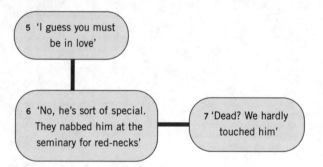

5 'I guess you must be in love'

6 'No, he's sort of special. They nabbed him at the seminary for red-necks'

7 'Dead? We hardly touched him'

Check your answers on page 55.

B Consider these issues.

a The effects of Isa's love for Andres on her relationship with Beto.

b Andres's attempts to resist the questioning.

c The effects on the reader of the graphic descriptions of torture.

d The different approaches of Hog and Snake.

e The character and background of Andres's rescuers.

CHAPTER 8 AND EPILOGUE

What finally unites
the crowd against
General
Zuckerman?

Most of the supporters of Miguel Alberti, the Silver Lion, have been rounded up and imprisoned. Francisco and Rosa manage to get Andres to the market place of San Miguel where Isa and Beto are giving a puppet show. Isa brings out the puppet of General Zuckerman, the unelected president, and a revolutionary mood grows in the crowd. As the police move in Isa and Beto

reach their van with the help of the market traders. What they do not know is that Andres is in the back of the van, helped there by Rosa. Beto and Isa drive out towards San José, stopping to picnic at the spot where they first met Andres. Beto discovers Andres in the van and together they go back to the river to surprise and delight Isa.

The Epilogue deals with the football match between Chile and England. At the match the American newspaper carrying the account of Don Chailey's disappearance is given to General Zuckerman. Also, leaflets showing the assassination of the Silver Lion, published by Diego, are handed out to the crowd. The Epilogue ends with the desperate attempts of the soldiers to destroy the leaflets.

FINAL TRIUMPH

COMMENT   The novel ends in hope rather than despair. The finer
parts of human life, love and companionship, have not
been destroyed. People rally round to help Andres, Isa
and Beto. The ordinary people in the market can see
through the lies of the government.

The Epilogue stresses the importance of the cultural
assistance given to Chile by Western Europe. England's
football match is potentially a great point of
propaganda for the government. It is totally ruined by
the leaflet distribution at the end.

GLOSSARY   **Villa Grimaldi** another cruelly ironic name for the House of
Laughter. Grimaldi was a famous clown

A *Identify the speaker.*

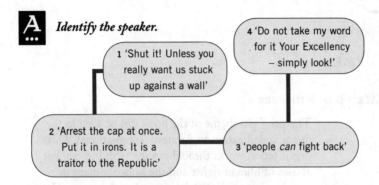

1 'Shut it! Unless you really want us stuck up against a wall'

2 'Arrest the cap at once. Put it in irons. It is a traitor to the Republic'

3 'people *can* fight back'

4 'Do not take my word for it Your Excellency – simply look!'

Identify the person 'to whom' this comment refers.

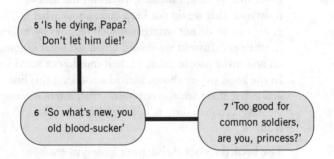

5 'Is he dying, Papa? Don't let him die!'

6 'So what's new, you old blood-sucker'

7 'Too good for common soldiers, are you, princess?'

Check your answers on page 55.

B *Consider these issues.*

a The relationship of the opening paragraph of Chapter 8 to the opening paragraphs of other chapters.

b The importance of the use of Juan's songs.

c The use of humour in the market scene.

d The location where Isa, Beto and Andres are reunited.

e The mood at the end of the story.

f The significance of the sporting contacts with Chile used in the Epilogue.

PART THREE

COMMENTARY

THEMES

TALKING IN WHISPERS

The main theme is opposition and resistance to a repressive government.

The principal theme of the book can be seen in the opening dedication to Amnesty International. This organisation works throughout the world to combat abuses of human rights and the imprisonment of people, often without trial, for political reasons. The book does not go into the reasons why such governments exist; instead it dwells on the idea of resistance, that we do not keep quiet about what is going on, we do not strengthen such regimes by 'talking in whispers'. Instead we should broadcast what is going on and make people aware of their murderous activities. In the book we are shown individuals taking this line of action but there are also reminders that, internationally, we have a human duty to oppose such inhuman regimes.

The book does not shrink from letting us see how difficult and dangerous opposition to this type of government is. They have no qualms about the use of violence, both publicly and privately. We see the treatment of Braulio and Don Chailey as well as the brutality against prisoners in the National Stadium. We find out that a government agent was able to kill the leader of the opposition in front of a packed election rally. Privately things are worse; Andres witnesses the sinister assassination of two truck loads of prisoners. He himself learns at first hand the horrors of physical torture and is finally dumped with a pile of corpses. More threatening is the fate of those such as Juan;

people who simply disappear and are never heard of again. There is no doubt as to the ruthlessness of the regime and the extremes of violence they will adopt in clinging to power.

Government tactics include violence and media propoganda.

Because this violence is seen and recognised as an element in government power, the population is held in the grip of fear and terror. Any opposition first has to conquer these psychological factors before progress can be made. We see how the crowd of Juan's neighbours are cowed and quiet while his house is ransacked with only the lone voice of the old Indian raised in opposition. Incidents like this remind us that opposition is just below the surface. In the scene in the market place at the end of the novel, it only takes a lone voice reacting to Isa's puppet of General Zuckerman to unleash the crowd's anger and scorn.

The government are also sustained by the use of media propaganda. After the assassination of Miguel, the radio station announces the cancellation of the elections and emphasises the lie that the Resistance movement is responsible for civil disorder and violence. The newspaper, *Mercury,* also publishes this story as well as a report on the ambush of Juan, and his character, which is totally at odds with the truth. At the end of the novel, the truth about Miguel and Don Chailey is only available through a foreign newspaper and leaflets printed on an illegal printing press.

Although the novel makes clear the power of this type of government, it does not see only despair in opposition to it. The novel has a positive message of hope. We see examples of spirit, courage, friendship and loyalty which are all seen to survive even amongst the violence and fear. They form the real core of resistance and examples will be given in the rest of this section.

YOUTH AND RESPONSIBILITY

In an interview with James Watson he talked of his motivation for writing *Talking in Whispers*. He mentioned his worries that today's teenagers are overtolerant, that they do not get angry at abuses of human rights and they do not seem to see the potential for resistance to repressive regimes or even repressive acts in their own country such as police action during the 1984–5 miners' strike. There is an overall mood of acceptance and no search for an alternative.

Compare the life of youngsters in Chile with that of British teenagers.

This identification of youthful mood and characteristics, found by James Watson in this country, is in direct contrast to that presented in the novel. Andres, Isa and Beto are about the same age as the general intended audience for the book. Most Western European teenagers should be immediately challenged by the circumstances facing the trio in Chile. Their first concerns are not chart music or which club to be seen in. They have lost their parents and are struggling to survive in a hostile environment. They do not accept the abuses of the regime; they get angry and resolve to resist it.

However, the writer does not make their situation so remote that Western European teenagers cannot empathise with them. As well as being physically beautiful, they are presented as being athletic and interested in sport. They enjoy music and Isa and Beto are involved in street theatre with their puppet show. Like so many young people today, Isa does voluntary work, helping out in a school for the children of those too poor to afford the state schools. More importantly, Andres and Isa fall in love and this arouses some tension in her relationship with Beto. What sustains them through the horrors is their friendship and loyalty, common among the best youthful attributes the world over.

Yet James Watson reminds us that youth cannot succeed on its own, no matter what the levels of energy and commitment. Don Chailey, Jack Normanton, Diego Rosales, Father Mariano and Sister Teresa are much older and wiser in the ways of the world, essential for the final triumph. But it is the optimism and energy of the youthful characters which pulls their efforts together and brings the final victory in the National Stadium.

CULTURAL AND CIVILISED VALUES

James Watson wants us to remember that, no matter how repressive a regime is of human rights, the best aspects of humanity will survive.

Note the importance of strong human qualities.

We have already mentioned the friendship and loyalty of Andres, Isa and Beto but there are other examples also in the novel. Jack Normanton does not forget his friend Don Chailey and keeps the potentially dangerous assignment with Isa to help. He is walking into the unknown but his loyalty to his colleague overcomes any fear. Diego is prepared to risk all to help Andres, the son of a co-musician of his cousin, Horacio. Father Mariano and Sister Teresa are well known as people who will help regardless of personal danger. The lady doctor puts her life in danger by coming to help them in treating Hernando Salas, the resistance leader. At the end of the novel Andres is rescued by little Rosa and her father Francisco even though they know from the fate of Rosa's brother, Tonio, what can happen to opponents of the regime. All of these provide examples of the best of human qualities surviving the darkest of human deeds.

A love of music and literature also survives and sustains people. The title of the book comes from a poem quoted by Isa as she re-emphasises her commitment to the publication of Don Chailey's photographs. Andres remembers the words of a song by Chico Buarque and some verses from Pablo Neruda as he first starts his search for Juan's friends.

Note the use of music as street theatre.

Music is also used to keep alive the memory of Juan throughout the novel. Although he is arrested at the start, taken to become one of the Disappeared, we are constantly reminded of him. James Watson based the character on Victor Jara, a famous Chilean singer who supported the government of Allende. After the military coup of 1973 he was arrested, tortured and murdered in the National Stadium with 5,000 other political prisoners. Beto is helped by singing one of Juan's songs as he drives away from the station after recovering the printing press. Juan's neighbours loved his singing and the group had an international reputation. His collection of books, burnt after his arrest, reveal a man who loved music and the work of radical writers.

An uplifting demonstration of the failure of the military junta to finish off the best attributes of the human spirit appears at the end of the novel. Beto and Isa are giving their puppet show, itself an example of the survival of creativity and escapist fun, in the market place of San Miguel. Isa brings out the puppet of General Zuckerman, the unelected leader of the military junta. The humour aroused in the crowd is as damaging as the bullets of the resistance fighters. The scorn and mockery brings the crowd together and Andres's escape is made easier. We have seen glimpses of the wealthy continuing their affluent lifestyle; the contemptuous humour of the ordinary people is a breath of fresh air in a dangerous world. Their spirits have not been crushed nor do they pretend that evil does not exist.

THE OUTSIDE WORLD

One of the themes of the book is the attitude of the outside world to regimes such as that of Chile. It is the actions of an American, Don Chailey, which bring about the final triumph, helped by another American, Jack Normanton. They are a reminder that not all American involvement is wrong. Through Juan's record and book collection we also see the importance of outside countries in keeping alive ideas, culture and hope.

The outside world is needed to help confront injustice.

The most graphic demonstration of international involvement comes in the Epilogue with the football match between England and Chile. We are left in no doubt that the ordinary Chilean loves football and would love to see the match. Juan had tickets for the whole group and Andres was looking forward to it. Yet we see that such sporting contacts are great propaganda achievements to governments such as the Chilean one in the novel. The government spokesmen are delighted by it and the attitude of the British ambassador is noteworthy. Overall the people would have been better off if other countries had denied Chile sporting contacts as Russia did in the run up to the 1974 World Cup. The isolation of South Africa proves the point; the worst excesses of the regime get international coverage and the moves to true democracy come about. James Watson wants us to ask why Western European governments, particularly Great Britain, treated Chile differently to South Africa.

Not only to ask ... but, as in the rest of the book, to get angry at the very existence of such a regime, to see it as an offence against the international community of humanity and decency.

STRUCTURE

The book has no great complicated or sophisticated structure. The events are told sequentially and cover a period of seven days. There is some use of flashback as Andres remembers his mother, her death and some incidents of family life. However, these memories are fitted naturally into the flow of the story, as Andres is waking up or walking along. In that way they add to the general air of realism in the story.

It is worth noting the pattern of using events in the National Stadium and other Security action at the start of most chapters. There is a direct comparison in mood between these settings in Chapter 1 and the Epilogue and the other chapters where they are used.

CHARACTERS

ANDRES

Andres is the central character in the book. He links the central events of the story and we see everything through his eyes.

When we first meet him he is a frightened youth, caught in an ambush by the Security forces which has seen his friend killed and his father arrested. Andres has little doubt as to the consequences of his father's arrest. We find out that he is sixteen, a good-looking, athletic youth with a keen interest in football. Certainly Isa is quickly attracted to him. He is still nervous and afraid in his first night with Isa and Beto where we find out about his family background. He is from a family with a history of opposition to the military junta, his father being a successful musician, his mother, Helen, a Scottish woman whose father had played football for Glasgow Celtic.

It is as he determines to spread the truth about the ambush on his father's group, 'Los Obstinados', that, by his own admission, his growing up process begins. We

Teenager
Attractive
Athletic
Brave
Resourceful
Loyal
Determined
Cultured
Symbol of hope for the future

have already seen, in his escape from the ambush, something of his innate physical courage and resourcefulness. This develops after his encounter with Don Chailey and his acquisition of the camera and films.

Although he finds willing allies in Isa and Beto, it is his determination which drives their plans along. Diego is his contact and it is Andres who has the most dangerous job at the station. He is in disguise with no acceptable back up story; the others are doing normal and explainable activities. Again, we see his resourcefulness as things start to go wrong with the plan. As they escape from the security van Andres is hiding in a wood with an illegal printing press, about to witness the sinister execution of prisoners, whilst Isa and Beto give a puppet show to schoolchildren. It is no wonder that his mental toughness and maturity develop so strongly. Yet he is aware of the value of friendship; he had seen himself as an outcast when he first set out on his mission but he is now fully involved in his friendship with Isa and Beto. He trusts them sufficiently to follow the advice of Beto and go to the seminary of Father Mariano.

After his capture we see the true spirit and courage of Andres. He is naturally frightened but he has enough mental alertness to remember his father's advice and try to work out strategies which will help him survive the torture. He knows he has to keep talking but give nothing away and we can see his mental agility as well as his mental courage in these scenes. What we see also is his physical courage. Despite appalling treatment and pain he gives nothing of value away. Indeed he frustrates his torturers to such an extent that he suffers more for it. Although he is fortunate with the death of Father Mariano we need to remember that his spirit was not broken by the torture; he survived mentally as well as physically.

The extent of his suffering is emphasised in the last chapter. Rosa and Francisco are shocked at his condition and he needs considerable help to get to Beto's van. But he gets his reward with his reunion with Isa, her love for him and their final triumph. He is presented as a model and noble youth, a reminder to Western European teenagers of his age of the challenges faced by teenagers in other parts of the world. He also reminds us of what can overcome these challenges; bravery, determination, loyalty and friendship. He is a direct contrast to the sinister men who run the junta – he is lively, attractive and open and a symbol of hope for people living under regimes such as those described in the book. If their future is to be built by young people such as Andres, and his friends, then they have nothing to fear and all to anticipate.

ISA

Although the younger of the twins, by a few minutes, Isa seems more mature than her brother, Beto, and often seems to take the lead and make the decisions. She is much more forward and decisive about the use of the General Zuckerman puppet; whilst Beto can only see the dangers, she can see the potential of scornful humour in their opposition to the regime. It is Isa who makes use of the lines from Chico Buarque's poem; she can see the need to cease 'talking in whispers' and to let as many as possible know the truth of what is going on in their country.

There is no doubt as to her physical beauty. Andres is quickly attracted to her 'Inca princess' looks and her attractions for the soldiers in the market place of San Miguel lets Beto's van escape a search and helps the escape of Andres. Yet she is also involved at the heart of the action – in the plan at the station and the escape, in the contacts with Sister Teresa to recover Don Chailey's possessions and in the meeting with Jack Normanton.

Teenager
Beautiful
Brave
Creative
Sensitive
Loyal
Symbol of women's
role in building
the future

Added to this combination of beauty and courage are her creativity and sensitivity. She is the creative force behind their street theatre puppet show and she shares Andres's love of music and poetry. She is aware of the effect her growing love for Andres is having on her relationship with her brother. Although she realises that she must have some life of her own she reassures her brother that she will always have time and love for him. Her love for Andres does develop and she has premonitions of his danger and suffering.

Like Andres, she is a symbol of hope for the future but with one important added dimension. She is a reminder of the role played by women in resistance movements such as those described in the book. This role is not just in the dangerous world Isa often sees but in the continuation of community activity which will be the foundations of a more just society; alongside her puppet theatre Isa helps out in a school for children too poor to afford state education. Her character is an important contrast to Andres, emphasising the importance of women in hope for the future.

BETO

Although Beto is the older of the twins he often grumbles about Isa being the more dominant. Yet we are given hints that Beto has been involved in resistance activity in the past; he knows that Andres will get help at the seminary of Father Mariano and he is aware of the possibilities for escape as they race away from the station pursued by the security van.

He is always there as solid support for Isa, driving the van and helping with the puppets. He is also a reminder of the penalties paid for opposition; the laundry where he worked was fire bombed for displaying a poster supporting the Silver Lion. He is loyal and totally devoted to his sister. He does feel pushed out by her growing love for Andres – he gives Andres the

Teenager
Brave
Loyal
Trusted friend
and brother

nickname of Towny which is a little scornful at first – but he would never stand in the way of her happiness.

Although he too enjoys music and poetry he is more of a man of action. Like the others he is a symbol of hope for the future. His particular importance is perhaps the idea of continuity; even when he thinks Andres is dead he talks of continuing the fight. He is a reminder that hope cannot be totally crushed and that the light of resistance will stay bright.

MINOR CHARACTERS

Diego Rosales

Diego is the cousin of Horacio, singer with Juan's group Los Obstinados. Diego was an old resistance fighter who had been imprisoned and tortured for supporting Allende. His cynical pragmatism is in contrast to the youthful enthusiasm of Andres, Isa and Beto. He never expected the elections to take place. But he has never given up the struggle and his printing press, hidden by old companions, is instrumental in the final triumph. He is an example of brave and defiant resistance to the evil and violence.

Don
Chailey/Jack
Normanton

These are both portrayed as brave and resourceful pressmen. They are determined to reveal the truth even though they are well aware of the dangers they face. Jack shows loyalty to his colleague in following him to Chile and bravery in going ahead with the secret meeting with Isa. They show that, no matter how strong and committed the resistance, it will still need help and support from outside its own country.

Father
Mariano

He is another member of the older resistance. Obviously his Seminary of Our Lady of Mercy has a history of helping resistance fighters. We find out that he is in ill health but he resists the torture in the House of Laughter without betraying anyone. His bravery allows Andres to escape with his life.

Sister Teresa   Another brave member of the seminary, who helps Hernando Salas and Isa. In the novel she is a reminder of the part played by women in the resistance and in building for the future.

Hog/Snake   The two interrogators of Andres who play out a sort of good cop/bad cop routine. They typify the servants of the junta as we see them in other parts of the novel; violent, intolerant and, in the case of Snake, mad and inhuman. Their viciousness and evil is a contrast to the brave and honourable behaviour of the people they torture.

LANGUAGE & STYLE

James Watson's book is aimed at a youthful audience, asking them to empathise with Andres, Isa and Beto and to get angry at regimes who abuse human rights. As such the language is accessible and straightforward, and easily understood by the target audience. However it is not totally plain. There are descriptive passages, especially where the writer reminds us of the beauty of the country. Dialogue is realistic and descriptions of character and city life are highly effective.

The style of the book is reminiscent of the journalism we might expect from Don Chailey or Jack Normanton. The action scenes move at a fast pace, particularly the escape from the central station. Tension is injected in the scene in the station and in the final escape from the market place with the intervention of the soldiers. Unnecessary background detail is cut out; for instance we do not see Jack Normanton's preparations to get to Chile, he simply appears in the story with his questions ready.

This style is very like television drama/documentary, particularly the genre of faction (see Literary Terms). This is a style based on real events and people but with some fictional material added. It is a highly effective method of reaching a mass audience on a topic which the mass media might not report with any depth or persistence. James Watson's book has a tele-visual style to it as it cuts dramatically from one scene to another but it gives sufficient emphasis to key thematic scenes such as the torturing of Andres.

PART FOUR

STUDY SKILLS

HOW TO USE QUOTATIONS

One of the secrets of success in writing essays is the way you use quotations. There are five basic principles:

- Put inverted commas at the beginning and end of the quotation
- Write the quotation exactly as it appears in the original
- Do not use a quotation that repeats what you have just written
- Use the quotation so that it fits into your sentence
- Keep the quotation as short as possible

Quotations should be used to develop the line of thought in your essays.

Your comment should not duplicate what is in your quotation. For example:

> Andres tells us that his mother was called Helen and that she was British. Also that her father played football for Glasgow Celtic. 'He glanced at the wrist watch given him by his British born mother, Helen. It had belonged to her Scottish father who had once – Andres never stopped boasting – played football for Glasgow Celtic.'

Far more effective is to write:

> Andres's watch was special to him as it had been a present from 'his British born mother, Helen'. He used to boast about the original owner, Helen's father, who 'had once ... played football for Glasgow Celtic'.

The most sophisticated way of using the writer's words is to embed them into your sentence:

> Isa, 'truly an Inca princess', managed to divert the soldiers with her beauty as she, with Beto, escaped from the market place.

When you use quotations in this way, you are demonstrating the ability to use text as evidence to support your ideas – not simply including words from the original to prove you have read it.

Everyone writes differently. Work through the suggestions given here and adapt the advice to suit your own style and interests. This will improve your essay-writing skills and allow your personal voice to emerge.

The following points indicate in ascending order the skills of essay writing:

- Picking out one or two facts about the story and adding the odd detail
- Writing about the text by retelling the story
- Retelling the story and adding a quotation here and there
- Organising an answer which explains what is happening in the text and giving quotations to support what you write

....

- Writing in such a way as to show that you have thought about the intentions of the writer of the text and that you understand the techniques used
- Writing at some length, giving your viewpoint on the text and commenting by picking out details to support your views
- Looking at the text as a work of art, demonstrating clear critical judgement and explaining to the reader of your essay how the enjoyment of the text is assisted by literary devices, linguistic effects and psychological insights; showing how the text relates to the time when it was written

The dotted line above represents the division between lower and higher level grades. Higher-level performance begins when you start to consider your response as a reader of the text. The highest level is reached when you offer an enthusiastic personal response and show how this piece of literature is a product of its time.

Coursework   Set aside an hour or so at the start of your work to plan
essay   what you have to do.

- List all the points you feel are needed to cover the task. Collect page references of information and quotations that will support what you have to say. A helpful tool is the highlighter pen: this saves painstaking copying and enables you to target precisely what you want to use.

- Focus on what you consider to be the main points of the essay. Try to sum up your argument in a single sentence, which could be the closing sentence of your essay. Depending on the essay title, it could be a statement about a character: We cannot doubt the courage of Andres as he endures horrific torture; an opinion about setting: The very existence of the House of Laughter represents the cruelty and evil of the regime; or a judgement on a theme: The theme of hope rather than despair runs through the story as we see so many examples of human love and friendship. The best of the human spirit is never crushed.

- Make a short essay plan. Use the first paragraph to introduce the argument you wish to make. In the following paragraphs develop this argument with details, examples and other possible points of view. Sum up your argument in the last paragraph. Check you have answered the question.

- Write the essay, remembering all the time the central point your are making.

- On completion, go back over what you have written to eliminate careless errors and improve expression. Read it aloud to yourself, or, if you are feeling more confident, to a relative or friend.

If you can, try to type your essay, using a word processor. This will allow you to correct and improve your writing without spoiling its appearance.

Examination The essay written in an examination often carries more
essay   marks than the coursework essay even though it is
               written under considerable time pressure.

               In the revision period build up notes on various aspects
               of the text you are using. Fortunately, in acquiring this
               set of York Notes on *Talking in Whispers*, you have
               made a prudent beginning! York Notes are set out to
               give you vital information and help you to construct
               your personal overview of the text.

               Make notes with appropriate quotations about the key
               issues of the set text. Go into the examination knowing
               your text and having a clear set of opinions about it.

In the   In most English Literature examinations, you can take
examination   in copies of your set books. This is an enormous
                advantage although it may lull you into a false sense of
                security. Beware! There is simply not enough time in an
                examination to read the book from scratch.

- Read the question paper carefully and remind
  yourself what you have to do.
- Look at the questions on your set texts to select the
  one that most interests you and mentally work out
  the points you wish to stress.
- Remind yourself of the time available and how you
  are going to use it.
- Briefly map out a short plan in note form that will
  keep your writing on track and illustrate the key
  argument you want to make.
- Then set about writing it.
- When you have finished, check through to eliminate
  errors.

To summarise, • **Know the text**
these are the • **Have a clear understanding of and opinions on the storyline,**
keys to success   **characters, setting, themes and writer's concerns**
                 • **Select the right material**
                 • **Plan and write a clear response, continually bearing the question**
                   in mind

A typical essay question on *Talking in Whispers* is followed by a sample essay plan in note form. This does not present the only answer to the question, merely one answer. Do not be afraid to include your own ideas and leave out some of the ones in this sample! Remember that quotations are essential to prove and illustrate the points you make.

Choose two or three instances in the novel where Andres is in danger. Write about what these events tell us of Andres's character. Look also at the language features in your chosen extracts.

Part 1
Beginning of
Chapter 1

Andres is frightened – he has lost his father and friends. He has enough determination and presence of mind to escape.
Use of verbs expresses urgency of situation. Dialogue snappy like the commands of the soldiers.

Part 2
At the railway
station

Andres more assured and grown up.
At the centre of the action and danger – he is the one in disguise.
Able to deal with things going wrong – ensures plan is completed.
Style is fast and pacy, reflecting the action but interruptions to the plan build up the tension.

Part 3
In the House of
Laughter

Andres in extreme danger – facing a horrific death.
Physically courageous as he withstands torture.
Mentally strong – thinks of strategies to avoid giving away vital information.

More importantly, at the end of it all he is badly damaged physically but his spirit is still alive and positive. Style is more drawn out reflecting Andres's ordeal – language reflects pain and inhumanity of torturers.

FURTHER QUESTIONS

Make a plan as shown above and attempt these
questions.

1 What evidence is there in the book that the people
of Chile can be hopeful about the future even
though the government in the novel is an evil one.

2 Write about the women characters in the book and
show how they are part of a positive message for the
future.

3 Write about the characters who give help to Andres,
Isa and Beto. Explain how this help enables them to
fulfil their ambitions.

4 Look at the parts of the book where we see
government servants (e.g. the army, the Security)
carrying out government policies. Contrast their
actions with the friendship of Andres, Isa and Beto.

PART FIVE

CULTURAL CONNECTIONS

BROADER PERSPECTIVES

If you have enjoyed *Talking in Whispers* then you may like *The Freedom Tree* (Gollancz, 1976), another book by James Watson. This time the setting is the Spanish Civil War, again with the emphasis on the struggle for freedom from tyranny.

The film *Missing* (1982) stars Jack Lemmon and Sissy Spacek and is available on video. It is an account of how an American journalist disappeared from his flat in Chile shortly after the military coup of 1973. The journalist's girlfriend and father eventually discover that he had been executed in the National Stadium.

The best information on Human Rights is available from Amnesty International, 99–119 Rosebery Avenue, London, EC1R 4RE. World Wide Web: http://www.oneworld.org/amnesty/.

The character of Juan is based on the poet and folk singer Victor Jara. A book on his life and songs, edited by Ted Dicks, is available from Elm Tree Books, no. 0241895200. Also on Victor Jara there is a video titled *Companero: Victor Jara of Chile* in which his English wife talks of his life and death. It is available from ETV, 247A Upper Street, London, N1 1RV. Also available from the same source is *Message from Chile* in which a British doctor tells of her torture by the military junta and *Venceremos*, an account of the struggles after the 1973 coup, including scenes from the funeral of Pablo Neruda.

black comedy literature in which potentially tragic or unpleasant situations are treated with a cynical amusement. The naming of the detention centre as the House of Laughter and the Villa Grimaldi are examples of this. It is only by taking refuge in this sort of desperate humour that humane people can cope with totally inhumane situations.

faction novels that are based on actual events; also called the non-fiction novel. The words fact and fiction are combined together in a word that indicates the combination of invention and fact. *Talking in Whispers* is an example of this type of novel.

metaphor a metaphor goes further than a simile between two different things or ideas by fusing them together. One thing is described as being another thing. In the torture scene Andres's body is pulled all over. 'He was a puppet, handled … by a mad operator'. ·

motif a motif is some aspect of literature which recurs frequently. The green panama hat which the Silver Lion throws into the crowd, to be caught by Beto, is a symbol of peace and is used to bring about the final triumph. The puppets are also a motif. They are there when Andres, Isa and Beto first meet and they are a symbol of resistance in the market place at the end.

personification a variety of figurative or metaphorical language in which things or ideas are treated as if they were human beings with human attributes and feelings. After Andres has witnessed the secret executions we are told that 'The breeze discovered tears in his eyes'.

simile a figure of speech in which one thing is said to be like another. Similes always contain the words 'like' or 'as'. When being tortured Andres imagines his mind as being inaccessible, 'Resting like a mouse in a hole'.

TEST YOURSELF (Chapters 1–2)
A 1 Andres *(Chapter 1)*
2 Beto *(Chapter 1)*
3 Hernandes, security chief *(Chapter 1)*
4 Newsreader *(Chapter 1)*
5 Andres *(Chapter 1)*
6 Araucanian Indian *(Chapter 2)*
7 Don Chailey *(Chapter 2)*

TEST YOURSELF (Chapter 3)
A 1 Officer in charge of book burning *(Chapter 3)*
2 Old Indian neighbour of Juan *(Chapter 3)*
3 Andres *(Chapter 3)*
4 Isa *(Chapter 3)*
5 Diego *(Chapter 3)*
6 Diego *(Chapter 3)*
7 Don Chailey *(Chapter 3)*

TEST YOURSELF (Chapters 4–5)
A 1 Station supervisor *(Chapter 4)*
2 Isa *(Chapter 4)*
3 Father Mariano *(Chapter 5)*

4 Doctor *(Chapter 5)*
5 Girls at train station *(Chapter 4)*
6 Andres *(Chapter 4)*
7 Father Mariano *(Chapter 5)*

TEST YOURSELF (Chapters 6–7)
A 1 Snake *(Chapter 6)*
2 Sister Teresa *(Chapter 6)*
3 Jack Normanton *(Chapter 7)*
4 Rosa *(Chapter 7)*
5 Isa *(Chapter 6)*
6 Andres *(Chapter 6)*
7 Father Mariano *(Chapter 7)*

TEST YOURSELF (Chapter 8 and Epilogue)
A 1 Francisco *(Chapter 8)*
2 General Zuckerman's puppet – General Zuckero *(Chapter 8)*
3 Isa *(Chapter 8)*
4 Director of State Information Services *(Epilogue)*
5 Andres *(Chapter 8)*
6 General Zuckero *(Chapter 8)*
7 Isa *(Chapter 8*

NOTES

NOTES

GCSE and equivalent levels (£3.50 each)

Harold Brighouse
Hobson's Choice

Charles Dickens
Great Expectations

Charles Dickens
Hard Times

George Eliot
Silas Marner

William Golding
Lord of the Flies

Thomas Hardy
The Mayor of Casterbridge

Susan Hill
I'm the King of the Castle

Barry Hines
A Kestrel for a Knave

Harper Lee
To Kill a Mockingbird

Arthur Miller
A View from the Bridge

Arthur Miller
The Crucible

George Orwell
Animal Farm

J.B. Priestley
An Inspector Calls

J.D. Salinger
The Catcher in the Rye

William Shakespeare
Macbeth

William Shakespeare
The Merchant of Venice

William Shakespeare
Romeo and Juliet

William Shakespeare
Twelfth Night

George Bernard Shaw
Pygmalion

John Steinbeck
Of Mice and Men

Mildred D. Taylor
Roll of Thunder, Hear My Cry

James Watson
Talking in Whispers

A Choice of Poets

Nineteenth Century Short Stories

Poetry of the First World War

FORTHCOMING TITLES IN THE SERIES

Advanced level (£3.99 each)

Margaret Atwood
The Handmaid's Tale

Jane Austen
Emma

Jane Austen
Pride and Prejudice

William Blake
Poems/Songs of Innocence and Songs of Experience

Emily Brontë
Wuthering Heights

Geoffrey Chaucer
Wife of Bath's Prologue and Tale

Joseph Conrad
Heart of Darkness

Charles Dickens
Great Expectations

F. Scott Fitzgerald
The Great Gatsby

Thomas Hardy
Tess of the D'Urbervilles

Seamus Heaney
Selected Poems

James Joyce
Dubliners

William Shakespeare
Antony and Cleopatra

William Shakespeare
Hamlet

William Shakespeare
King Lear

William Shakespeare
Macbeth

William Shakespeare
Othello

Mary Shelley
Frankenstein

Alice Walker
The Color Purple

John Webster
The Duchess of Malfi

Future Titles in the York Notes Series

Chinua Achebe
Things Fall Apart

Edward Albee
Who's Afraid of Virginia Woolf?

Jane Austen
Mansfield Park

Jane Austen
Northanger Abbey

Jane Austen
Persuasion

Jane Austen
Sense and Sensibility

Samuel Beckett
Waiting for Godot

John Betjeman
Selected Poems

Robert Bolt
A Man for All Seasons

Charlotte Brontë
Jane Eyre

Robert Burns
Selected Poems

Lord Byron
Selected Poems

Geoffrey Chaucer
The Franklin's Tale

Geoffrey Chaucer
The Knight's Tale

Geoffrey Chaucer
The Merchant's Tale

Geoffrey Chaucer
The Miller's Tale

Geoffrey Chaucer
The Nun's Priest's Tale

Geoffrey Chaucer
The Pardoner's Tale

Geoffrey Chaucer
Prologue to the Canterbury Tales

Samuel Taylor Coleridge
Selected Poems

Daniel Defoe
Moll Flanders

Daniel Defoe
Robinson Crusoe

Shelagh Delaney
A Taste of Honey

Charles Dickens
Bleak House

Charles Dickens
David Copperfield

Charles Dickens
Oliver Twist

Emily Dickinson
Selected Poems

John Donne
Selected Poems

Douglas Dunn
Selected Poems

George Eliot
Middlemarch

George Eliot
The Mill on the Floss

T.S. Eliot
The Waste Land

T.S. Eliot
Selected Poems

Henry Fielding
Joseph Andrews

E.M. Forster
Howards End

E.M. Forster
A Passage to India

John Fowles
The French Lieutenant's Woman

Elizabeth Gaskell
North and South

Oliver Goldsmith
She Stoops to Conquer

Graham Greene
Brighton Rock

Graham Greene
The Heart of the Matter

Graham Greene
The Power and the Glory

Thomas Hardy
Far from the Madding Crowd

Thomas Hardy
Jude the Obscure

Thomas Hardy
The Return of the Native

Thomas Hardy
Selected Poems

L.P. Hartley
The Go-Between

Nathaniel Hawthorne
The Scarlet Letter

Ernest Hemingway
A Farewell to Arms

Ernest Hemingway
The Old Man and the Sea

Homer
The Iliad

Homer
The Odyssey

Gerard Manley Hopkins
Selected Poems

Ted Hughes
Selected Poems

Aldous Huxley
Brave New World

Henry James
Portrait of a Lady

Ben Jonson
The Alchemist

Ben Jonson
Volpone

James Joyce
A Portrait of the Artist as a Young Man

John Keats
Selected Poems

Philip Larkin
Selected Poems

D.H. Lawrence
The Rainbow

D.H. Lawrence
Selected Stories

D.H. Lawrence
Sons and Lovers

D.H. Lawrence
Women in Love

Laurie Lee
Cider with Rosie

Christopher Marlowe
Doctor Faustus

Arthur Miller
Death of a Salesman

John Milton
Paradise Lost Bks I & II

John Milton
Paradise Lost IV & IX

Sean O'Casey
Juno and the Paycock

George Orwell
Nineteen Eighty-four

John Osborne
Look Back in Anger

Wilfred Owen
Selected Poems

Harold Pinter
The Caretaker

Sylvia Plath
Selected Works

Alexander Pope
Selected Poems

Jean Rhys
Wide Sargasso Sea

William Shakespeare
As You Like It

William Shakespeare
Coriolanus

William Shakespeare
Henry IV Pt 1

William Shakespeare
Henry IV Pt II

William Shakespeare
Henry V

William Shakespeare
Julius Caesar

William Shakespeare
Measure for Measure

William Shakespeare
Much Ado About Nothing

William Shakespeare
A Midsummer Night's Dream

William Shakespeare
Richard II

William Shakespeare
Richard III

William Shakespeare
Sonnets

William Shakespeare
The Taming of the Shrew

William Shakespeare
The Tempest

William Shakespeare
The Winter's Tale

George Bernard Shaw
Arms and the Man

George Bernard Shaw
Saint Joan

Richard Brinsley Sheridan
The Rivals

R.C. Sherriff
Journey's End

Muriel Spark
The Prime of Miss Jean Brodie

John Steinbeck
The Grapes of Wrath

John Steinbeck
The Pearl

Tom Stoppard
Rosencrantz and Guildenstern are Dead

Jonathan Swift
Gulliver's Travels

John Millington Synge
The Playboy of the Western World

W.M. Thackeray
Vanity Fair

Mark Twain
Huckleberry Finn

Virgil
The Aeneid

Derek Walcott
Selected Poems

Oscar Wilde
The Importance of Being Earnest

Tennessee Williams
Cat on a Hot Tin Roof

Tennessee Williams
The Glass Menagerie

Tennessee Williams
A Streetcar Named Desire

Virginia Woolf
Mrs Dalloway

Virginia Woolf
To the Lighthouse

William Wordsworth
Selected Poems

W.B. Yeats
Selected Poems

York Notes – the Ultimate Literature Guides

York Notes are recognised as the best literature study guides.
If you have enjoyed using this book and have found it useful, you
can now order others directly from us – simply follow the ordering
instructions below.

HOW TO ORDER

Decide which title(s) you require and then order in one of the following
ways:

Booksellers
All titles available from good bookstores.

By post
List the title(s) you require in the space provided overleaf,
select your method of payment, complete your name and
address details and return your completed order form and
payment to:

> *Addison Wesley Longman Ltd*
> *PO BOX 88*
> *Harlow*
> *Essex CM19 5SR*

By phone
Call our Customer Information Centre on 01279 623923 to
place your order, quoting mail number: HEYN1.

By fax
Complete the order form overleaf, ensuring you fill in your
name and address details and method of payment, and fax it
to us on 01279 414130.

By e-mail
E-mail your order to us on awlhe.orders@awl.co.uk listing
title(s) and quantity required and providing full name and
address details as requested overleaf. Please quote mail
number: HEYN1. Please do not send credit card details by
e-mail.

York Notes Order Form

Titles required:

Quantity	Title/ISBN	Price

Sub total _____

Please add £2.50 postage & packing _____

(P & P is free for orders over £50) _____

Total _____

Mail no: HEYN1

Your Name _____

Your Address _____

_____

Postcode _____ Telephone _____

Method of payment

☐ I enclose a cheque or a P/O for £_____ made payable to Addison Wesley Longman Ltd

☐ Please charge my Visa/Access/AMEX/Diners Club card
Number _____ Expiry Date _____
Signature _____ Date _____

(please ensure that the address given above is the same as for your credit card)

Prices and other details are correct at time of going to press but may change without notice. All orders are subject to status.

☐ *Please tick this box if you would like a complete listing of Longman Study Guides (suitable for GCSE and A-level students)*

🌀 York Press

🔲 Longman

Addison
Wesley
Longman